Short Sharp Shakespeare Stories

Hamlet

Retold by Anna Claybourne

Illustrated by Tom Morgan-Jones

First published in paperback in 2016
Copyright © Wayland 2016

Wayland, an imprint of
Hachette Children's Group
Part of Hodder & Stoughton
Carmelite House
50 Victoria Embankment
London EC4Y 0DZ

Editor: Elizabeth Brent
Design: Amy McSimpson
Illustration: Tom Morgan-Jones

Dewey number: 823.9'2-dc23

10 9 8 7 6 5 4 3 2 1

ISBN: 978 0 7502 8117 1

Library eBook ISBN: 978 0 7502 9368 6

Printed in (...
An Hachett ... UK company
www.hache ...te.co.uk
www.hache ... drens.co.uk

CONTENTS

INTRODUCING *HAMLET*

Shakespeare is famous as one of the greatest writers who ever lived, and *Hamlet* is considered by many to be his greatest play. It's still often performed regularly – and the role of Hamlet himself is one of the biggest challenges an actor can take on.

Who was Shakespeare?

William Shakespeare was a playwright (author of plays) in London, England just over 400 years ago. He wrote dozens of plays for his theatre company to perform, and sometimes worked as an actor too. Though his language now sounds old-fashioned, his stories are still as popular as ever.

What's the story?

Prince Hamlet of Denmark is in turmoil after his father's death - especially as his mother, Gertrude, has suddenly married the new king, Hamlet's slimy uncle Claudius. After his father's ghost appears and tells Hamlet that Claudius murdered him, Hamlet vows to take revenge - but how, and when? In a fragile mental state, can he do the right thing, or is he doomed for disaster?

Read on to discover the strange, harrowing and heartbreaking story of *Hamlet*.

Hamlet: Who's who?

Every Shakespeare play starts with the *dramatis personae,* or list of characters.

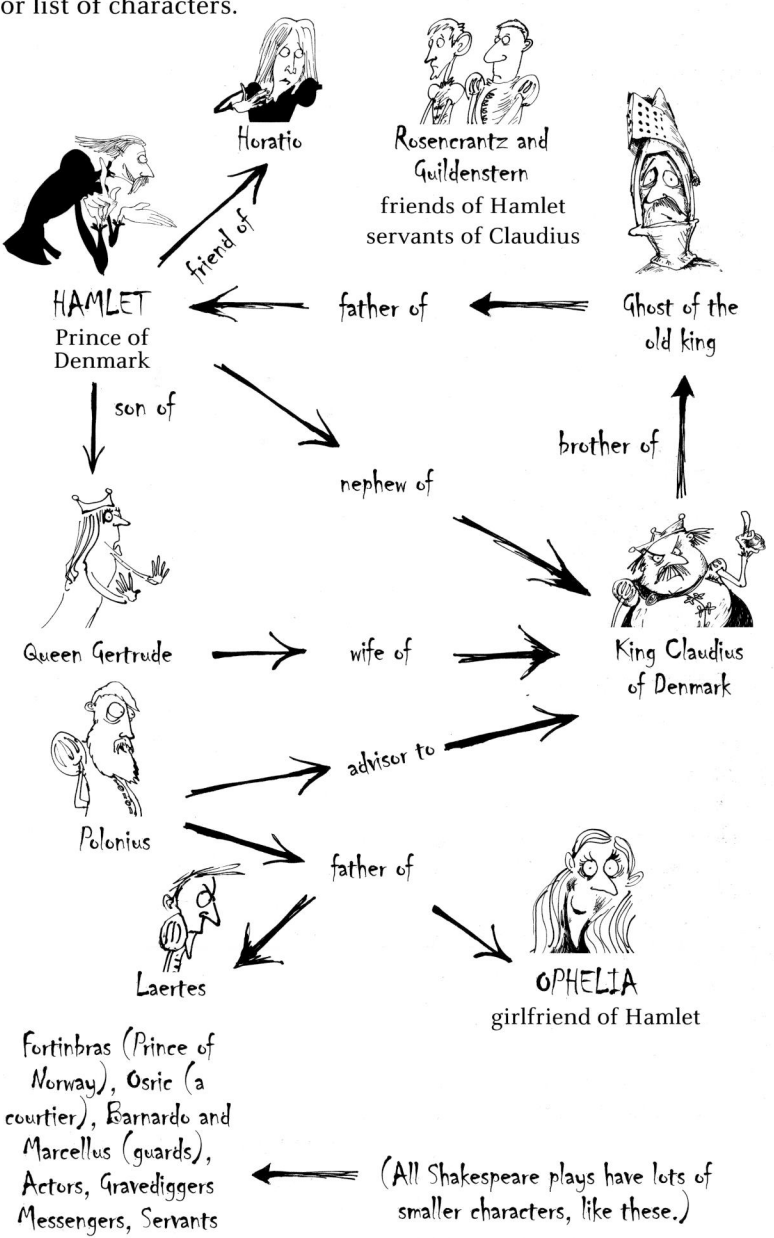

Horatio

Rosencrantz and Guildenstern
friends of Hamlet
servants of Claudius

HAMLET
Prince of Denmark

friend of

Ghost of the old king

father of

son of

nephew of

brother of

Queen Gertrude

wife of

King Claudius of Denmark

advisor to

Polonius

father of

Laertes

OPHELIA
girlfriend of Hamlet

Fortinbras (Prince of Norway), Osric (a courtier), Barnardo and Marcellus (guards), Actors, Gravediggers Messengers, Servants

(All Shakespeare plays have lots of smaller characters, like these.)

Chapter One

It was almost midnight, and Elsinore Castle, Denmark's royal palace, stood in darkness. High on the battlements, Barnardo, a palace guard, gazed out over the sea, and waited. He had asked another guard, Marcellus, to meet him there, and to bring Horatio, a friend of Prince Hamlet himself. There was something they wanted him to see.

"Barnardo?" a voice called out of the darkness.

"Marcellus! Over here! Is Horatio with you?"

"Yes, he's here." Marcellus and Horatio emerged from the shadows. "Have you seen it yet?"

"No, not yet."

"Horatio says we're imagining it," Marcellus said, "but this time, when the ghost comes, he'll see it for himself."

"Come on, guys," Horatio laughed. "There isn't a ghost!"

"There is!" said Barnardo. "Last night, we were standing right where we are now, and– "

"Shhhh!" Marcellus broke in. "It's right there!"

A pale human figure was materialising in front of them, becoming more solid as they watched.

Barnardo whispered: "And it looks just like the dead king. Don't you think?"

"It... it does!" Horatio gulped. "In his armour!"

What does that mean!?
"Mark it" means notice it,
or look at it closely.

7

"Talk to it," Marcellus said.

"Erm..." Horatio began, nervously. "Who are you? You look like His Majesty, our king, who died just last month. Speak to me, ghost!"

The ghost turned away, and began to fade. "Talk to us!" Horatio called after it. "How can we help you? Do you have something to tell us?" But the ghost was gone.

"I think you annoyed it," said Marcellus.

"But at least you believe us now!" said Barnardo.

"If I hadn't just seen it with my own eyes, I wouldn't," said Horatio, still trembling. "But I have. And I'm sure it's a bad sign. We know Prince Fortinbras of Norway wants to attack Denmark – what if this ghost came to warn us of disaster?"

"If only it would tell us!" said Marcellus.

"I know what to do," said Horatio. "I'll ask Hamlet to come up here tomorrow night. If the ghost is the dead king, then surely he'll speak to his own son."

Prince Hamlet was miserable. His father had only been dead a month, and he was still grieving. But every day, he had to face his smug, self-satisfied Uncle Claudius, who now sat on the throne.

To make things worse, Claudius had also married Queen Gertrude, the dead king's wife and Hamlet's own mother. Couldn't they have waited a while?

And for that matter, couldn't Claudius stop going on about how great he was – just for a second? Hamlet sighed. He was doing it right now.

"Of course, we all miss my brother, the old king," Claudius was announcing to his assembled lords and servants, and his loyal advisor Polonius. "But life goes on! Gertrude is my wife now..." – Claudius broke off to give Gertrude a sickly smile – "and what better way to get over the sadness of the funeral, than with a lovely wedding?" Hamlet rolled his eyes.

"Anyway," King Claudius went on, "down to business. I'm well aware of the threat to Denmark from that young upstart, Prince Fortinbras. So I'm sending a letter to his uncle, the King of Norway, to ask him to put a stop to it. That should do the trick!" Claudius signed and sealed the letter, and gave it to his messengers to deliver at once.

"Right, what's next?" said Claudius. "Ah yes, Laertes. You wanted to see me."

Laertes was the son of Polonius, the King's right-hand man. He had been away at university in France, but had returned for the funeral, coronation and royal wedding.

"I was wondering if I could go back to my studies in France, Your Majesty," asked Laertes politely.

"If your father consents, then of course," said Claudius. Laertes bowed.

"And now, we turn to Hamlet," said Claudius, in a patronising voice. "Hamlet – your mother and I do wish you would stop being so gloomy."

"Yes, dear," said Gertrude. "I'm sorry your father died, but people do die, you know. Maybe it's time to move on, and not seem so miserable all the time."

Hamlet burned with indignation, but kept his cool.

"I'm sorry if I seem unhappy, Mother," he said.
"But that's how I feel."

What does that mean!?
Claudius says Hamlet has clouds hanging on him as a way of describing his bad mood.

"Well, the time for mourning is over," Claudius declared.
"I'm your father now – as well as your uncle, and your king."

Hamlet could have punched him. But he did nothing. Soon,
he could return to university himself, in Wittenberg, and
escape from it all.

"Oh, and about your studies," said Claudius, as if reading his
mind. "You're not going back. We think you should stay here
and play your proper role, as Prince of Denmark." And they
swept out of the room.

How Hamlet wished none of this had happened. How he wished he could just die, rather than have to hear Claudius's smug voice in his ears.

How could Gertrude have replaced his father so easily? It made Hamlet furious. It broke his heart. But there was nothing he could do.

"Hamlet?" It was his friend Horatio, with two of the castle guards. "Are you OK?"

"Yes, yes, I'm fine. Well, maybe I'm feeling a bit muddled up, what with a funeral, a coronation AND a wedding to attend, so close together."

"I'm sorry about your father, Hamlet," said Horatio kindly.
"He was a great man."

"Yes," Hamlet said. "We won't see his like again."

"Hamlet," Horatio said. "We came to tell you something.
We think we did see your father. Last night, on the battlements.
We saw his ghost."

"It's true, sir," said Marcellus. "I've seen it three times."

Hamlet stared at them. "Did – did you talk to it?"

"I tried," Horatio said, "but it won't answer me."

"Then I'll watch with you tonight," said Hamlet.
"In case it comes back."

Meanwhile, Laertes went to say farewell to his sister, Ophelia.

"Write to me!" he said. "And Ophelia – about Hamlet. I know you've always liked him, and you two are very close. But he's a prince, and he has bigger things to think about. Don't give away your heart to him. I don't want you to get hurt."

Ophelia did love Hamlet, and hoped he would marry her one day. But she didn't argue. "You behave yourself too," she smiled.

"Laertes is right," said her father Polonius, coming in. "Don't make a fool of yourself, Ophelia. Stay away from Hamlet."

"I'll obey your wishes, father," Ophelia said.

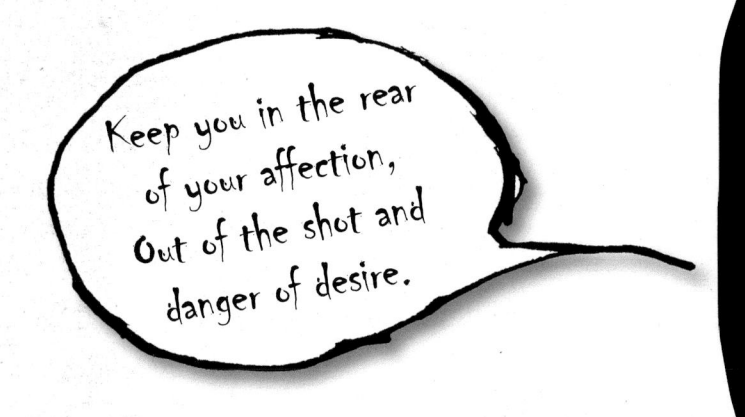

Keep you in the rear of your affection, Out of the shot and danger of desire.

What does that mean!?
Laertes tells Ophelia to hold back her affection for Hamlet, in order to avoid the problems caused by falling in love.

Hamlet shivered as he waited on the battlements with Horatio and Marcellus. "It's cold tonight," he said. "What time is it?"

"I heard the midnight bell," said Marcellus. "The ghost usually appears around now."

"Hamlet – look." Horatio was pointing along the walkway. And as Hamlet peered, he saw the ghostly form take shape.

It was his father – in full battle armour, but with his visor up, so Hamlet could see his face. As he looked more closely, he saw that the ghost's eyes were sad, and seemed to be beseeching him.

Hamlet felt his heart thumping in his throat.

"F-father," he began. "Why are you here? Why have you left your peaceful grave? Talk to me."

The ghost said nothing, but reached out a hand, and beckoned Hamlet towards it.

"It wants you to follow it!" whispered Horatio.

"Don't go!" Marcellus blurted out, grabbing Hamlet's arm. "It's a ghost!"

"What do I have to fear?" asked Hamlet calmly. "Let me go." He walked steadily towards the ghost. It led him on, along the moonlit walkway, until his friends were left far behind.

"Stop," said Hamlet. "I've come far enough. What do you have to say?"

17

What does that mean!?
"Foul" means evil. By "unnatural", the ghost means against nature, because Claudius killed his own brother.

Murder most foul... cruel and unnatural!!

The ghost stopped at last, and began to speak.

"Listen carefully, Hamlet," it said, "for I do not have much time. If you ever loved your father..."

"I did," said Hamlet, feeling tears in his eyes.

"... then avenge his murder."

"Murder!?"

"You think I died from a snake bite, as I slept in the orchard, don't you?" said the ghost. "Everyone in Denmark thinks that. But they're wrong. The snake that killed me lives, and wears my crown."

"My uncle?" Hamlet gasped.

"Yes, Claudius, that sneaking, smiling villain. He loved my wife, and wanted my throne – so while I slept, he poured deadly poison in my ear. That's how I died, and as my son, you must avenge me. Don't harm the Queen – take your revenge on Claudius." The ghost began to fade away.

"Father...!"

"Goodbye, Hamlet. Remember me!"

Horatio and the guards came running up to Hamlet. "What happened?" gabbled Marcellus.

"It did speak to me," said Hamlet. "But you must swear you'll never tell a soul what we saw here."

Chapter Two

Hamlet had no idea what to do. He wanted to take revenge, as his father had asked. But that would mean killing Claudius. How could he kill the King? And how could he be sure he really had seen a ghost, and that its words were the truth?

Hamlet didn't want anyone to find out what he knew, or what he was planning. So he decided to behave as strangely as possible. If Claudius thought he was insane with grief, he wouldn't see him as a threat.

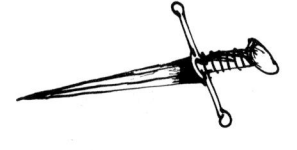

In his rooms in the palace, Polonius was talking to a servant when Ophelia ran in, looking terribly upset.

"Father!" she cried. "I've just had such a fright! I've been avoiding Hamlet, like you told me to. But just now, when I was sewing in my room, he came in, uninvited – and he was in such a state! He was all pale, his shirt was unbuttoned, and he didn't even have any trousers on! – and his stockings were dirty and fallen down around his ankles!"

"Oh my goodness," exclaimed Polonius in shock. "What did he do to you, my dear!?"

"Nothing – well, he grabbed my arm, then just stared at me for a long time. Then he left."

"Oh dear," Polonius fretted. "Perhaps my advice was unwise. The poor man has gone insane with love for you! We must go and see Claudius, and explain that Hamlet has lost his mind."

What does that mean!?
"Affrighted" means frightened.

Meanwhile, Claudius had sent for two of Hamlet's old schoolfriends, Rosencrantz and Guildenstern.

"Hamlet isn't quite himself these days," the King began. "Of course, his father's death has upset him, but it's more than that. He's in a very odd mood."

"We thought maybe you could spend some time with him," said Queen Gertrude. "See if you can find out what's wrong."

"And whatever you discover," Claudius added, "come and tell me."

When Rosencrantz and Guildenstern had gone, Polonius came in.

"Your Majesty!" He bowed deeply. "I have news! Firstly, from Norway. Fortinbras has called off his attack on Denmark, on the condition we let him march across our kingdom to attack Poland."

"Excellent!" said Claudius. "And secondly?"

"Ah yes, Your Majesty. It's Hamlet. I think he's gone insane."

"Well, that's not really news," said Gertrude.

"No, no, there's more, my Queen. I think I know the reason. It's all my fault. Hamlet loves my daughter, Ophelia. I was worried for her, and told her to keep away from him. That's what's driven him mad – he loves Ophelia, but she's been ignoring him."

"But how can we be sure?" said Claudius.

"I have a plan, sir. I'll arrange for Hamlet to bump into Ophelia in the hallway, while you and I hide behind a curtain. We'll listen to their conversation, and you'll see what I mean."

"My friends, what brings you here?" asked Hamlet, when Rosencrantz and Guildenstern found him.

"We just thought we'd visit you," said Rosencrantz. But Hamlet wasn't stupid. "Come on," he said. "Who sent you?"

Rosencrantz and Guildenstern looked embarrassed.

"OK, I'll say it, so you don't have to. The King sent you, to find out what's wrong with me. Well, you can tell him I don't feel great. Everything seems pointless to me. Laughter, sunshine, having fun – even love – I'm not interested in them any more. So there's your answer."

"Aren't you interested in seeing plays, either, then?" asked Rosencrantz. "We've just seen a troupe of actors on their way to the palace to put on a show for us. That might cheer you up!"

"In fact, I think that's them arriving now," said Guildenstern. Polonius pompously led the troupe into the great hall, with their piles of props and costumes.

Hamlet pretended to find it all very dull. But as soon as Polonius was gone, he went to speak to the actors' leader.

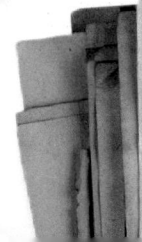

"Sir," he said, taking him aside, "Do you know the play *The Murder of Gonzago*?"

"Certainly, Your Highness", said the man.

"Great," said Hamlet. "Could you perform that for us all this evening? And if I wrote a few extra lines for it, you could learn them and put them in?"

"No problem at all, Your Highness," said the actor.

Hamlet planned to change the play so that it showed a king being murdered by having poison poured in his ear. If he saw Claudius looking guilty or alarmed, he would know the ghost's tale was true.

What does that mean!?
"Of late" means recently, "wherefore" means why, and "mirth" means sense of humour.

Chapter Three

"Well?" asked Claudius. "What did you find out?"

"It's hard to say," began Rosencrantz. "He says he's unhappy – but he won't say why."

"Oh dear," said the Queen. "If only he would take an interest in something."

"Well, luckily, Your Majesty, a troupe of actors have arrived, and Hamlet does seem very interested in them," Rosencrantz replied. "He's helping them prepare their show, and he wants us all to watch it this evening."

"Well, that's good news, at least," said the King. "A little entertainment for us all!"

That afternoon, as he had promised, Polonius told Ophelia to wait in a hallway, where Hamlet would bump into her.

As she read a book, Polonius and Claudius hid behind a wall-hanging, out of sight.

Soon enough, Hamlet came along. He was talking to himself, and he seemed to have a lot to say.

"To be, or not to be?" he pondered. "Is it better to endure all life's hardships – or to die, and leave them all behind?

"Dying's just like a sleep, really. But sleep means dreams – and what if they were bad dreams? What if you have nightmares after you die – never-ending nightmares?

To be or not to be? That is the question.

What does that mean!? In this famous quotation, Hamlet wonders if it is better to be alive or dead.

"Maybe that's why we're all afraid of dying. It's like a country no visitor ever returns from, and no one knows what it's really like. In the end, we're all cowards when it comes to death.

"But look, it's Ophelia," he said, spotting her. "How are you, Ophelia? Are you beautiful and good?"

Ophelia blushed. "What do you mean, Hamlet?"

"I used to love you, Ophelia," Hamlet said.

"I thought you did, too," she replied.

"Well, you're a fool, because I didn't really," Hamlet said rudely. "Most people are lying cheats, including me."

Ophelia tried not to cry.
"OK, I'm a fool,"
she said.

"And really, you shouldn't want to get married and have babies, and make more lying, cheating human beings. In fact, I think you should become a nun."

Ophelia couldn't stand it any more. "What's wrong with you!?" she screamed. "You used to be so nice! Why can't you go back to how you were!?" But Hamlet walked away.

As soon as he had gone, Claudius and Polonius tumbled out from behind the curtain.

"You know, Polonius, I don't think he's simply love-sick," said the King. "It's as if he's making this madness up. He's hiding something, I'm sure of it."

"You may be right," Polonius nodded wisely.

"I know," said Claudius. "I'll send Hamlet on a trip to England. That's what he needs – some fresh sea air. And it will get him out of the way."

"But first," said Polonius, "let's see if the Queen can get any sense out of him – tonight, after the play. I'll hide in her room, so I can listen in."

It was almost time for the performance, and everyone began making their way to the great hall. Hamlet went over to talk to Horatio.

"Horatio, I know I can trust you," said Hamlet, "and I need your help. I've changed the play, so that when the king dies, it will be the same way my father died – according to what the ghost told me. At that moment, watch Claudius carefully. We need to see if he starts or jumps, or looks guilty."

"I'll do the best I can," Horatio promised.

The King and Queen came in and sat down, along with Ophelia. The play began.

It told the story of a loving King and Queen, who had been married for 30 years. The King was getting old, but the Queen told him that if he died, she would never marry again.

The King decided to have a nap. He lay down to sleep in an orchard, decorated with paper flowers.

The Queen went away, and a man sneaked up to the sleeping King. He lifted the crown from the King's head, and put it on himself. Then he took out a tiny bottle, and poured the contents into the King's ear. He crept away, and the Queen came back to find her husband dead.

Claudius was getting up, unsteadily. "What's wrong, dear?" asked the Queen.

"Stop the play," Polonius said.

"Light the lamps!" shouted Claudius. "I've had enough of this!" He stumbled out of the hall, followed by Gertrude, Polonius and all his courtiers. The actors stared in confusion.

Hamlet looked at Horatio. "Did you see that?"

"I did!" said Horatio. "He certainly seemed upset!"

Rosencrantz and Guildenstern came back in. "Hamlet, the Queen wants to see you," said Guildenstern. "She's in her bedroom."

Claudius quickly summoned Rosencrantz and Guildenstern. "This is getting serious," he said. "Hamlet is raving mad, and could be dangerous. I'm sending him to England first thing tomorrow. I want you to go too, and keep an eye on him."

As soon as Claudius was alone, he fell to his knees. "What have I done!?" he sobbed. "My crime stinks to high heaven, and I'm sure Hamlet has sniffed it out! I should pray for forgiveness – but how can I pray, when I've been so evil? What can I say? 'Dear God, I've murdered my brother, but I'm really sorry'? It's hopeless! I wish I could undo it all!"

Shaking, he closed his eyes, and tried to pray, as hard as he could. At that moment, Hamlet passed the open doorway and saw him.

"I could kill him now," Hamlet said to himself. "It would be easy." He pulled his dagger out. "But if I do it while he's praying, he'll go to heaven! That wouldn't be fair. No – I'll wait until he's fallen asleep after drinking too much, or something like that." He walked on to his mother's room.

Hamlet strode in. "What do you want, Mother?"

What does that mean!?
Claudius describes his crime as
"rank", or rotten, and smelling bad.

"You've upset the King, Hamlet," Gertrude said.

"I've upset the King!?" Hamlet said, flabbergasted. "What about what you did to the old king, my father? You and Claudius were in love, and saw each other behind his back. Didn't you?"

Gertrude couldn't deny it, but she didn't want to hear it, either. "How dare you!" she cried. "I'll fetch the guards!"

Of course, the Queen was not alone. As Polonius had planned, he was in her room too, eavesdropping while hidden by a wall hanging. When he heard Gertrude getting upset, he panicked. "Help, help!" came his muffled shout from behind the tapestry.

How now, a rat?

"What, is that murdering rat here, too?" Hamlet shouted. He grabbed his dagger and plunged it through the cloth. Polonius slumped to the ground.

"Hamlet – what have you done?" Gertrude gasped.

"I've killed the King, just as he killed my father," said Hamlet. Gertrude looked completely confused, and Hamlet realised she hadn't known about the murder. He pulled back the tapestry.

"Polonius!?" Hamlet gasped. "I thought that was Claudius!"

Then he saw the ghost again, right there in his mother's room. "Father!?" he whispered.

"Remember your purpose, Hamlet!" warned the ghost. "Punish Claudius, not your mother!"

"What are you looking at!?" said Gertrude.

"It's my father! Can't you see him?" Hamlet said, as the ghost faded away once again.

But Gertrude hadn't seen anything. "Help!" she wailed. "Hamlet's completely lost his mind!"

"Don't worry about me, Mother," Hamlet said. "I'm off to England, and then I'll be out of your way. I'm sorry about Polonius. Excuse me." And he left the room, dragging Polonius's body with him.

Chapter Four

Gertrude hurried to find her husband to tell him what had happened. Claudius was horrified.

"That dagger was meant for me!" he gulped. "I knew Hamlet was dangerous. This is all my fault, my dear," he went on. "I should have dealt with Hamlet's illness sooner. I only didn't because I love him like a father, and wanted him to get better."

Claudius called Rosencrantz and Guildenstern, and told them to take Polonius's body to the chapel. But although they found Hamlet himself, the body was nowhere to be seen. Hamlet insisted on seeing Claudius.

"OK, Hamlet," said Claudius. "Where have you put Polonius?"

"He's at dinner, Your Majesty."

"What are you talking about?"

"He's at dinner, sir, but he's not the one enjoying a feast. The worms are eating him!" Hamlet smirked.

"Tell me where he is!"

"I can't tell, but you may smell," Hamlet riddled. "Have a sniff about in the upstairs hallway."

"Go, quickly," Claudius instructed his men. "The body's upstairs."

"There's no rush," said Hamlet. "He's not going anywhere."

Claudius scowled. "Hamlet, this has gone too far," he said. "You'll leave for England right now. It's for your own safety – you must go before word of this gets out. As your father, I just want to protect you."

"Of course, how kind," said Hamlet sarcastically. "Well, I'm ready."

What does that mean!?
Claudius asks how Hamlet is, and Gertrude compares his craziness to the waves and the wind battling each other in a sea storm.

Claudius gave Rosencrantz and Guildenstern a letter for the English king, and they led Hamlet to the castle harbour, where a ship was waiting.

Once he was alone, Claudius sighed with relief. "I know the English king fears Denmark's power," he said to himself, "and he'll do as I ask – have Hamlet killed immediately."

As Hamlet reached the docks, he saw another ship moored in the harbour – a Norwegian ship. It was Prince Fortinbras of Norway and his army, on their way to attack Poland. Hamlet could hear Fortinbras talking to his captain, telling him to go and ask King Claudius for safe passage through Denmark.

"Why I can't I be like Fortinbras?" Hamlet mused. "He hardly stops to think – he just takes action."

Hamlet knew he had delayed too long. He must take revenge on Claudius, one way or another – and soon.

Back in Elsinore, Gertrude had something else to worry about. Ophelia was already upset by Hamlet's behaviour, but when she heard that he had killed her father Polonius, she went insane with grief. She wandered through the castle in her nightgown, staring vacantly, and singing songs of death. Gertrude called Claudius to see the sad scene for himself.

"The poor girl," Claudius sighed. "First Hamlet goes mad, then Polonius is killed, and now this! And to top it all, Laertes has heard about his father's death, and he blames me! He's on his way back from France right now. What a mess!"

"What shall we do about Ophelia, Your Majesty?" asked Horatio.

"Keep an eye on her," said Claudius. Ophelia wandered away, with Horatio following. Moments later, Laertes rushed in, his sword in his hand. He marched up to Claudius.

He is dead and gone, lady,
He is dead and gone
At his head a grass-green turf
At his heels a stone

What does that mean!?
Ophelia sings about a grave, with a stone surrounded by green grass.

41

"WHAT happened to my father?" he roared in Claudius's face.

"He's dead, Laertes. I'm sorry."

"But Claudius didn't kill him!" Gertrude added.

"Then who did?" Laertes demanded. "Because I want revenge!"

"Calm yourself, Laertes," Claudius soothed. "I'm as upset as you are over the loss of your dear father. Let me explain – "

Just then, Ophelia came back. She had been in the garden. Her bare feet were muddy and she was carrying armfuls of dead flowers. As she sang her strange, sad songs, she handed flowers to Gertrude and Claudius. Everyone stared at her.

"Ophelia..." Laertes gasped, but she ignored him. "What have you done to her? Ophelia!"

Still singing, Ophelia headed out of the room.

"Do you see the state she's in?" Laertes shouted.

"Laertes, let me help you," said Claudius, taking him aside. "I'll explain everything, and if you want revenge, why, it will be yours."

43

The next day, two messengers came to Horatio, saying they had letters for him and the King.

Horatio opened his letter, and read:

My dear Horatio,
I am back in Denmark, in hiding. My ship was attacked by pirates, and I took the chance to leap onto their ship. My ship sailed away, with Rosencrantz and Guildenstern still on board, and the pirates brought me home. Come and see me – these men know where to find me. But first, be sure to let them deliver my letter to the King.
Your friend,

Hamlet

Meanwhile, Claudius was talking to Laertes. He explained how Hamlet had killed Polonius, but couldn't be punished, for fear of upsetting Gertrude. He was about to tell Laertes how he had got rid of Hamlet, when the messengers arrived.

"A letter from Hamlet, Your Majesty."

Claudius stared. "Hamlet?" He opened the letter.

Your Royal Highness,
I have returned to your kingdom. Tomorrow I'll meet with you, and explain how I made my way home.

Hamlet

"I – I thought I had sent Hamlet away for good – but he's come back..!" Claudius told Laertes.

"Well, that suits me," growled Laertes. "It's my chance for revenge."

"Of course," said Claudius, starting to smile. "I have an idea, Laertes. You must challenge Hamlet to a duel. But we'll swap your blunt fencing blade for a sharpened one, so you can kill him. It will look like an accident."

What does that mean!?
Gertrude describes how Ophelia fell, clutching her garlands of flowers.

"I'll make sure of it by dipping the blade in poison," said Laertes.

"And as a back-up plan, I'll have a poisoned drink ready for him too," said Claudius.

"Claudius! Claudius!" Gertrude ran in, sobbing. "Ophelia is dead!"

"My sister?" Laertes gasped.

"She ran off again, and climbed the willow tree that leans over the river. She fell in, and her nightgown weighed her down, and got tangled among the weeds. That's where we found her. Ophelia has drowned."

"Drowned...?" Laertes wanted to cry, but he stopped himself. "This is all Hamlet's fault," he snarled. "And I will get my revenge."

When down her weedy trophies and herself fell in the weeping brook.

Chapter Five

In the chapel churchyard, the gravediggers were hard at work.
Polonius's funeral was only just over, and now they were digging
a grave for Ophelia. As they worked, they joked and sang songs.
Though they dug up old bones and even skulls from the soil,
death didn't bother them. They were used to it.

When the grave was almost ready, one of the gravediggers went
to fetch a drink, while the other had a rest. At that moment, along
came Hamlet and Horatio, who had arranged to meet away from
the castle.

Hamlet asked who the grave was for, but the gravedigger would only say it was for a woman.

"Or a body, who was once a woman," the gravedigger went on. "Look at all these old bones. They were all people once. Look, here's a skull that's been here for years. The old joker!" He pulled a grubby skull from the soil.

"How do you know whose it is?" asked Hamlet.

"Because of where we buried it," said the gravedigger. "That's Yorick, the old king's clown."

"Yorick!" Hamlet took the skull, and turned it around in his hands. "I remember him! He always made me laugh when I was little. He was so funny. Look, there's no laughing now. He doesn't even have lips any more."

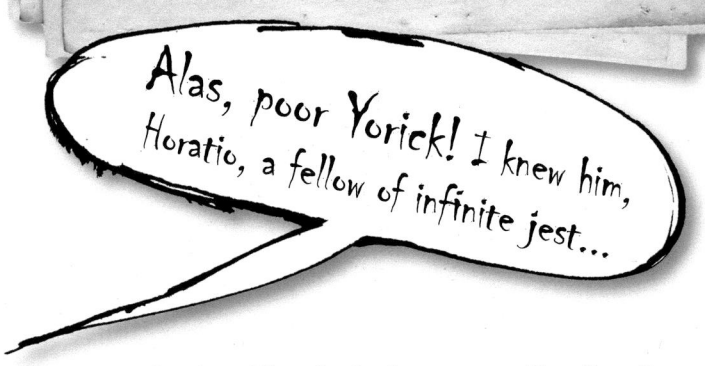

What does that mean!?
Hamlet describes Yorick as a man of "infinite jest", or endless humour.

Alas, poor Yorick! I knew him, Horatio, a fellow of infinite jest...

Someone was coming. They looked up to see Claudius, Gertrude and Laertes leading a funeral procession.

"What's Laertes doing here? Let's watch," said Hamlet, stepping behind a large gravestone.

The coffin-bearers brought the coffin up to the grave.

"Lay my sister in the ground," said Laertes sadly. "Let flowers grow where she lies."

"It's Ophelia?" Hamlet whispered, horrified. "Ophelia has died?"

The coffin was lowered down, and the gravediggers stood ready to fill the grave. But Laertes could not bear it. "Wait! One last goodbye," he cried. He jumped down into the grave, and kissed the coffin. "How I loved you, Ophelia."

51

"No, I loved her," Hamlet shouted, striding out of his hiding place. He jumped into the grave and pushed Laertes aside.

"Hamlet!" cried Gertrude. "You're back!"

"You!" Laertes snarled. "You evil murderer!" He threw himself at Hamlet and grabbed him around the throat, trying to strangle him.

"Get your hands off me," Hamlet panted. "I loved her more than forty thousand brothers could."

This infuriated Laertes, and the two men rolled to and fro as they wrestled inside the grave, until Claudius ordered his men to pull them out and separate them.

"That's enough!" he said sternly. "Let us bury poor Ophelia in peace. We will sort this matter out later."

"So, I've already told you about the pirates, in my letter," Hamlet said to Horatio, once they were alone again. "But there's something else. Before they attacked us, I waited until Rosencrantz and Guildenstern were up on deck, and checked through their bags. There I found a letter from Claudius to the English king, telling him I'd gone crazy, and to kill me as soon as we arrived!"

"No!" said Horatio. "Really?"

"Here it is," said Hamlet, taking the letter from his pocket.

"You stole it?"

"I replaced it," Hamlet explained. "I wrote another letter, in the same handwriting, and instead of my name, I wrote Rosencrantz and Guildenstern."

"Unlucky for them," said Horatio.

"It serves them right, for obeying Claudius," said Hamlet. "Now I know for sure about all the evil things he's done, I'm determined to kill him, and avenge my father. The first chance I get."

A courtier named Osric came in. "Your Highness, Prince Hamlet," he said. "You're wanted in the great hall. Laertes has challenged you to a duel, and the King is placing bets. He thinks you'll win."

Hamlet sighed. He might as well get this out of the way first.

"Shake hands, gentlemen," Claudius instructed. The hall was prepared for a duel, with the fencing swords laid ready. On a side table stood a goblet, containing the drink Claudius had prepared for Hamlet. Gertrude and all the lords and courtiers sat and watched, while Osric was to be the referee.

"I'm sorry, Laertes," Hamlet said as they shook hands. "I was unwell, and I didn't mean to kill your father. I'm as upset about Ophelia as you are."

"Let the duel decide our argument," said Laertes, coldly. But he was starting to feel guilty.

"Give them the swords," Claudius called, and the match began.

Hamlet was an excellent fencer, and before long, his blunt blade struck Laertes.

"One hit!" called Osric. "Round two!"

Hamlet won the second round as well. He got the feeling Laertes wasn't fighting as well as he could.

"Well done, Hamlet!" Gertrude shouted. "I'll drink to your success!"

She picked up the goblet.

"Gertrude, don't drink that!" said Claudius quickly. But she had already taken a big glug.

"Round three!" called Osric.

"Come on Laertes, I'm not a baby," Hamlet said, as they faced each other. "Fence properly."

"Fair enough," said Laertes, and suddenly lashed out at Hamlet. The sharpened blade cut his shoulder. Hamlet fought back so hard that both swords were knocked to the ground, and as the duellers scrambled to pick them up, they were swapped around.

Hamlet saw terror in Laertes' eyes as he swiped at him again, and was surprised to see blood on his shirt, too. The sword had scratched him.

"The Queen!" cried Osric. Gertrude had fallen to the floor.

"She's just fainted because of the blood," Claudius explained.

"No – I've been poisoned! The drink!" Gertrude choked, then closed her eyes. She was dead.

No, no, the drink, the drink! – O my dear Hamlet! The drink, the drink! I am poisoned...

"What's going on!?" Hamlet asked, as everyone stared silently. "Osric, lock the castle doors." Osric ran off.

"Who here has done this?" Hamlet demanded.

"Hamlet, save your breath," groaned Laertes, sinking into a chair. "You're a dead man, and so am I. My sword was poisoned, and it's cut us both. The drink was poisoned too. The King's to blame."

"Then I hope there's some poison left," said Hamlet. He turned, strode up to Claudius, and stabbed him with the sword.

"Help!" Claudius squealed. "Servants, save me!" But everyone stood stock-still.

"A drink, Claudius?" said Hamlet. He grabbed the poisoned goblet, forced Claudius's mouth open and sloshed the deadly drink in. A minute later, Claudius lay dead, beside his wife.

"Hamlet, I'm sorry too," Laertes said quietly. "Let us forgive each other." They were his last words.

The rest is silence.

Hamlet felt the poison creeping around his heart, and his legs going numb. He fell to his knees.

"Horatio," he groaned. "I'm dying... Tell the people of Denmark what happened here."

"I'd rather join you in death," said Horatio sadly. He picked up the goblet. "There's a drop of this left."

"No!" gasped Hamlet, using his last ounce of strength to reach over and smash the goblet to the floor.

Osric ran back into the hall. "Hamlet, Horatio!" he said. "Fortinbras has returned from Poland! He and his men are coming!"

"Then let Fortinbras rule Denmark," Hamlet whispered, "the rest is silence." His head sank to the ground, and he lay still.

What does that mean!?
Hamlet's last words say that he cannot speak any more, as he is about to die.

HAMLET AT A GLANCE

What makes *Hamlet* so famous and admired? As well as being Shakespeare's longest play, it is his most detailed exploration of the mind. Hamlet is often described as dithering his way through the whole play. But it is through this dithering that Shakespeare reveals the fears, uncertainties and torments of being human.

Hamlet as a play

Hamlet is one of Shakespeare's tragedies – he also wrote comedies and history plays. Like his other tragedies, it focuses on bad decisions that lead to a disastrous ending. Though this book retells it as a story, it was written as a play, made up of lines of dialogue (the speech of the characters), and a few stage directions (instructions for the actors).

Here is part of a scene from *Hamlet* as Shakespeare wrote it:

ACT 1

Scene IV.

A tempestuous noise of thunder and lightning heard.

Enter Hamlet, Horatio and Marcellus. ← Stage directions

HAMLET: The air bites shrewdly. It is very cold.

HORATIO: It is a nipping and an eager air.

HAMLET: What hour now?

HORATIO: I think it lacks of twelve.

MARCELLUS: No, it is struck.

FACT FILE:

FULL TITLE: *The Tragedy of Hamlet, Prince of Denmark*

DATE WRITTEN: around 1601

LENGTH: 4,024 lines

Acts and scenes

Like all Shakespeare plays, *Hamlet* has five main sections, or acts. They are divided into shorter sections, called scenes, each with its own setting. Acts and scenes help actors to learn their lines, and also give structure to the play.

THE FIVE ACTS OF *HAMLET*

ACT 1 (5 scenes)

As Hamlet mourns his dead father, who has been replaced by his Uncle Claudius, he meets his father's ghost, who says Claudius murdered him. Hamlet must avenge his death.

ACT 2 (2 scenes)

Hamlet pretends to be mad to avoid suspicion. He rewrites a play as a test to see if Claudius did kill his father.

ACT 3 (4 scenes)

Hamlet decides Claudius is guilty, but misses a chance to kill him, instead killing Polonius, his adviser, by mistake.

ACT 4 (7 scenes)

Claudius sends Hamlet to England, but he escapes and returns. Meanwhile Ophelia, Polonius's daughter, goes mad and dies, and her brother Laertes vows revenge on Hamlet.

ACT 5 (2 scenes)

Claudius sets up a duel to help Laertes kill Hamlet. But the plan goes wrong, and almost everyone ends up dead.

THE STORY OF *HAMLET*

Shakespeare didn't usually make up the plots of his plays. Instead, he borrowed stories from old books, myths and legends, or from real-life history. He often wove them together or changed parts of them to make an exciting play.

The Tale of *Hamlet*

Hamlet is based mainly on a story from medieval Denmark about a prince called Amleth. It appears in a 13th-century book on Danish history, and was also retold in a popular French version written in 1570. This was when Shakespeare was at school, so he might have read it when he was young.

In these early versions, Amleth succeeds in killing the King and taking the throne. Shakespeare changed this happy ending to turn the story into a tragedy. Over time, Amleth's name also changed, becoming Hamblet, and finally Hamlet.

The Ur-Hamlet

Shakespeare's *Hamlet* is thought to have been written around 1601. However, experts think that an earlier play about Hamlet also existed, as reports from the time mention it being seen at the theatre in the 1590s. This mysterious version, now lost, is known as the "Ur-Hamlet" ("ur" means original). Maybe it was by another playwright. Or it could even have been an earlier version of the play by Shakespeare himself.

I'm sure I can jazz this up a bit!

The real Hamlet

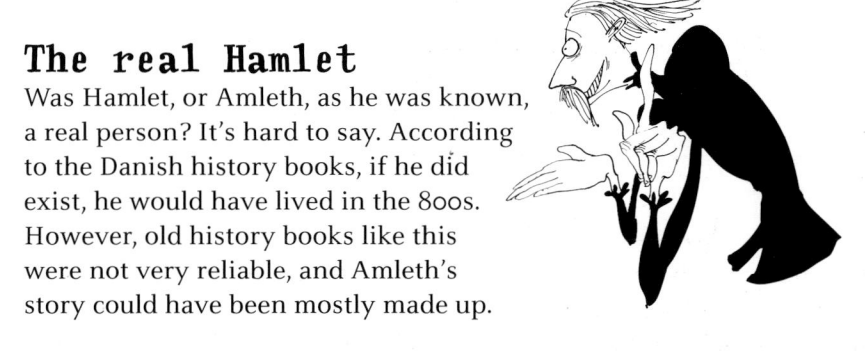

Was Hamlet, or Amleth, as he was known, a real person? It's hard to say. According to the Danish history books, if he did exist, he would have lived in the 800s. However, old history books like this were not very reliable, and Amleth's story could have been mostly made up.

Elsinore (or Helsingør in Danish) is, on the other hand, a real place in Denmark. It was known in Shakespeare's time as the site of a large royal castle, where Shakespeare set the action.

SHAKESPEARE AND *HAMLET*

Why did Shakespeare write *Hamlet*? Firstly, it was his job – he had to keep coming up with new, exciting works to keep his theatre company in business. There may also have been personal reasons behind his choice of story.

Hard at work

If Shakespeare wrote *Hamlet* around 1601 as experts think, it was a busy time for him. He had left his home town of Stratford to work as an actor and writer in London. In 1594, he joined a new theatre company, The Lord Chamberlain's Men.

The Globe

By 1600, the company had become a great success. Shakespeare had written several hit shows for them, and they had even built their own London theatre, the Globe. They needed a steady supply of new plays to put on.

A spectacle on stage

To pull in the crowds, Shakespeare often based his plays on well-known stories. He knew the tale of *Hamlet* was popular and his audience would be familiar with it. It was a bit like film-makers today turning a bestselling book into a movie. By making it a tragedy, he also guaranteed lots of gory murders, which theatre-goers liked to see!

Star vehicle

Shakespeare almost certainly wrote the detailed, complex character of Hamlet for the company's star actor, Richard Burbage – just as movie roles are written for top film stars today. Burbage was famous for his sensitive, emotional performances and ability to remember lines perfectly.

Richard Burbage

Hamlet and Hamnet

Some people think there may be a connection between *Hamlet* and the loss of Shakespeare's 11-year-old son, Hamnet, who had died in 1596. Shakespeare also had a friend called Hamnet, and in those days "Hamlet" was an alternative spelling of the name.

Maybe thinking about his son inspired Shakespeare to study the story of "Hamblet". The play also explores feelings of grief, which Shakespeare must have experienced.

STAGING *HAMLET*

The Lord Chamberlain's Men performed their plays both indoors, in royal palaces or law schools, and at open-air theatres, such as the Globe.

The Globe Theatre

The Globe was The Lord Chamberlain's Men's own theatre, which they built in 1599. It was ring-shaped, with roofed galleries around an open-air standing area in front of the stage. This layout was based on Ancient Greek and Roman theatres. Greek and Roman plays, myths and architecture were all very fashionable in Shakespeare's time. Today, there's a replica Globe in London, which shows Shakespeare's plays.

Going to the Globe

At the Globe, plays were performed in the afternoon. They needed daylight, as there were no electric lights, and candles couldn't light up such a large theatre. All the actors were male – boys with higher voices played female characters. Audience members often chatted and heckled, enjoyed snacks and drinks during the show, and even threw food!

Special effects

Theatre companies at the time didn't use much scenery, but they did make an effort to create special effects that would thrill the audience. For example, there were trap doors in the stage that could be used to make characters appear and disappear suddenly. They would probably have been used for the ghost scenes in *Hamlet*.

Stars of the stage

Shakespeare's company included some major theatre stars that audiences flocked to see. Richard Burbage usually played starring roles, like Hamlet or Macbeth. There were also comic actors such as Will Kempe and Robert Armin, who were usually given their own special parts. In *Hamlet*, they would have played the gravediggers.

Macbeth

A female Hamlet!

Soon after Shakespeare's time, women did start acting on the stage. In the late 1700s, theatre legend Sarah Siddons even played Hamlet herself!

HAMLET:
THEMES AND SYMBOLS

In many of Shakespeare's plays, you can find themes, ideas and images that repeat themselves through the play. They emphasise what the play is about and give it a strong atmosphere. Here are some of the main themes and symbolic images in *Hamlet*:

Uncertainty

Hamlet contains many situations where it is impossible to know something for certain, or to be sure of the right path. Is it better to live or to die? To take action at once – or to wait? Is the ghost real or imagined? Is Hamlet really insane, or just pretending?

This is also reflected in objects, such as the sealed letter given to Rosencrantz and Guildenstern, and the tapestries and wall hangings that characters hide behind. The play looks at how the truth can be unclear.

Death and the afterlife

For Hamlet, the greatest uncertainly of all is death, and what might happen after we die. He ponders these mysteries in several speeches. The play shows us what happens to bodies after death, as the gravediggers bring bones out of the ground and Hamlet examines them. It also includes Hamlet's father's ghost, a dead man's spirit who cannot rest.

Ears and hearing

Ears are very important in Hamlet. First, the ghost tells how Claudius killed him by pouring poison in his ear, and this image is repeated in the actors' show. It symbolises, or stands for, the lies and deception that Claudius has spoken to those around him, and the lies that other characters tell each other. Characters also often eavesdrop on each other, hiding out of sight, but listening intently.

Pretending

Hamlet is full of people putting on acts and pretending to be something they are not. Claudius pretends to be a rightful king, and Gertrude pretends to be an innocent bystander. Rosencrantz and Guildenstern pretend to be Hamlet's concerned friends, when they are actually the King's spies. Most famously of all, Hamlet pretends to be insane, but his fake madness gets horribly out of hand. The play-within-a-play is another symbol of the layers of role-playing and pretending in human relationships.

INSANITY

Shakespeare's plays, especially his tragedies, often explore insanity – people going crazy, why this happens and what madness is like. It plays a big part in *Macbeth* and *King Lear* as well as *Hamlet*, but in *Hamlet* it is explored most deeply.

What is madness?

Famously, Hamlet decides near the start of the play that he will pretend to be insane. He acts like a madman in front of Ophelia and other characters, but we also see him speaking normally to Horatio, and making long, thoughtful speeches to himself – suggesting he is still sane.

This contrasts with other characters' madness. Ophelia loses her mind with grief, and her insanity leads to her death. Claudius presents himself as a perfect king, but he has actually murdered his own brother to grab the throne – he's power-crazed.

The play asks: What does it mean to be mad? How do we know someone is mad? Does "insanity" just mean a different point of view from your own? Or is everyone actually a bit crazy, in their own way?

One of the gravediggers says Hamlet will fit right in in England, because everyone is crazy there!

He shall recover his wits there, or, if he do not, it's no great matter there.

The four humours

In Shakespeare's time, people saw mental health differently from today. Humans were said to have four "humours" or substances in their bodies: blood, yellow bile, black bile, and phlegm. If they were out of balance, it could cause problems or personality changes. Too much black bile caused "melancholy", making you indecisive and gloomy, like Hamlet. Today, he might be described as "depressed".

Treating insanity

In the 1600s, the modern medicines we have today didn't exist. But there were traditional herbal medicines, such as St John's wort, which has been used since ancient times to treat "nerves" – meaning mental or emotional problems.

Mentally ill people usually had to be cared for at home, and would be prayed for. There were some charity hospitals run by Christian communities that would take in mentally ill people and look after them. Bedlam in London, a home for the insane from around 1400, was the most famous.

71

THE LANGUAGE OF *HAMLET*

Shakespeare was a poet as well as a playwright, and he wrote
his plays in very poetic language, with regular rhythm
or meter, and striking images, patterns and descriptions.
They help to conjure up vivid scenes and emotions, and
reflect the personalities of individual characters.

Everyday speech

In some scenes, Shakespeare uses prose speech – normal,
everyday language that is not in a regular meter. It's often used
for the speech of servants and working-class people, especially
when they speak to each other.

FIRST GRAVEDIGGER:
Who builds stronger than a mason,
a shipwright or a carpenter?

SECOND GRAVEDIGGER:
When you are asked this
question next, say "a grave-
maker". The houses that he
makes last till doomsday.

Did you know?

Shakespeare was the first to write down
many words and phrases which we still
use today. In *Hamlet*, they include

mind's eye, barefaced, and outbreak.

Blank verse

Most of *Hamlet*, like other Shakespeare plays, is written in blank verse, a kind of non-rhyming poetry with five beats per line. It is used for formal situations and for the speech of wealthy or aristocratic characters. This example of blank verse is from Hamlet's famous "To be, or not to be?" speech:

Hamlet: **To be, or not **to be? That is the question –
Whether 'tis nobler in the mind to suffer
The *slings and arrows of outrageous fortune,
Or to take arms against *a sea of troubles,
And, by opposing, end them?

.... To die, **to sleep,
**To sleep, perchance to dream.

Assonance: Groups of words with similar sounds, like "struts" and "frets".

Alliteration: Pairs or patterns of words with the same first letter.

** Repetition: Repeating a word or phrase creates an echoing rhythm to reinforce an idea.

* Metaphors: Something is described as something else – for example, the random events of fate are described as weapons (slings and arrows), and a mass of troubles are a "sea".

73

WHAT *HAMLET* MEANS NOW

Although *Hamlet* is long, complex and sometimes hard to understand, it is still probably Shakespeare's best-known, most quoted and most performed play. The role of Hamlet is seen as a great test of an actor's skill, and theatre companies put on new stage productions every year, all around the world.

Adaptation

Like many other Shakespeare plays, *Hamlet* isn't just performed as a stage play. It's also been made into films, animations, opera, ballet and comic books. Writers often copy elements of the plot of *Hamlet* when creating new works, such as Disney's *The Lion King*. And it has also inspired spin-offs, like the modern play *Rosencrantz and Guildenstern are Dead* by Tom Stoppard.

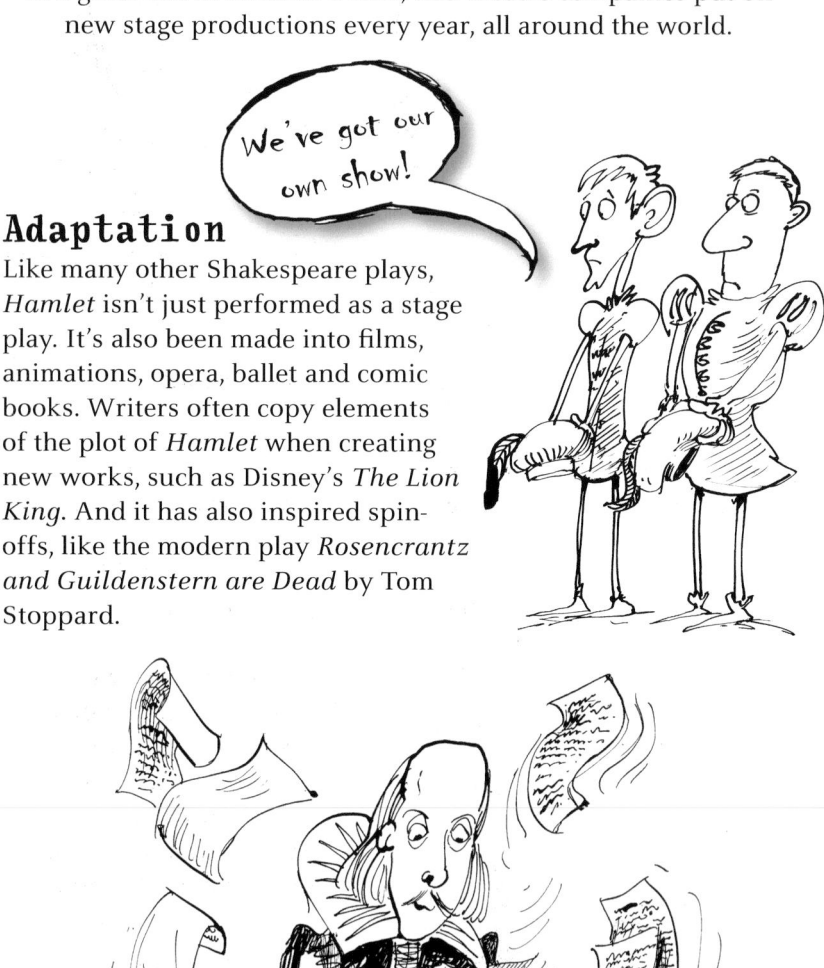

A man for all time

Why have Shakespeare's works survived for so long, and why do they still have so much meaning for us, 400 years later? Soon after his death, another writer, Ben Jonson, wrote about Shakespeare that, "He was not of an age, but for all time." He meant that the situations and ideas Shakespeare wrote about are universal – they apply to everyone. Even after all this time, we can still relate to the dilemmas and emotions of his characters.

What a great guy!

Ben Jonson

* For example, *Hamlet* deals with mental illness, grief and depression – things that affect people now as much as ever.

* *Hamlet* also explores the fear and mystery of death. No matter how long humans exist, that never changes.

* It's also easy to identify with another key theme in *Hamlet* – the fakeness and pretending that play a part in so many human relationships. Whether in the playground, at work or in families, we all still have to learn to deal with this.

SHAKESPEARE: HIS LIFE AND TIMES

For a large part of Shakespeare's life he lived and worked in London, but he was actually born in Stratford-upon-Avon, 160km (100 miles) away, in 1564.

Shakespeare's family

When Shakespeare was just 18, he married a lady named Anne Hathaway, who was eight years older than him. Together, they had three children, Susanna, the oldest, and Judith and Hamnet, who were twins. Sadly, Hamnet died in 1596, aged 11. While Shakespeare spent much of his life working in London, his family stayed in Stratford-upon-Avon. Shakespeare often visited Stratford and in 1597, he had earned enough money from his career to buy a big, grand house there, called New Place, for his family to live in.

Going home

Shakespeare finally retired and moved back to Stratford to live at New Place, probably in 1610 – around the same time that he wrote *The Tempest*. He still went on trips to London, and had many friends there, but no longer lived there.

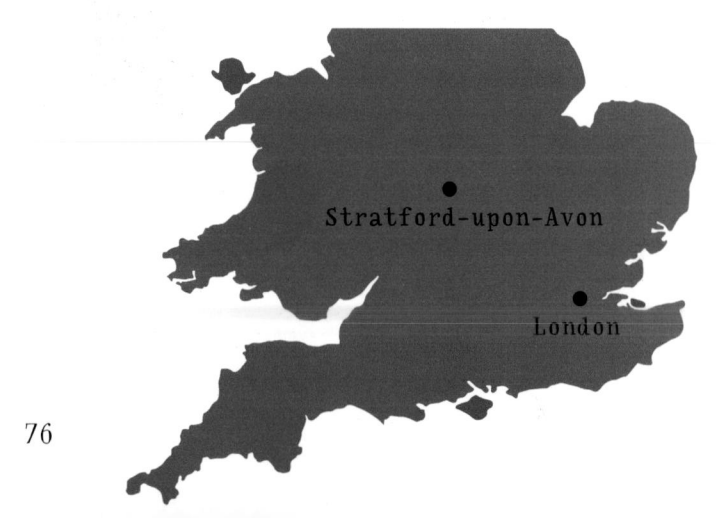

Stratford-upon-Avon

London

The lost years

Between 1585 (when Judith and Hamnet were baptised in Stratford) and 1592 (when Robert Greene, a London critic, called him an 'upstart crow') there is no trace of Shakespeare or his whereabouts at all. Historians have many theories about where he was and what he was doing at this time, but the most likely answer is that he was learning to be a playwright.

Last works

The Tempest was not actually Shakespeare's last play – he went on to write three more. But these last works were collaborations, written with another playwright, John Fletcher. They are *The Two Noble Kinsmen, Henry VIII*, and *Cardenio*.

Though records show the King's Men (as The Lord Chamberlain's Men became known) performed *Cardenio* in 1613, this play was lost long ago and no one knows what was in it. But maybe there's still a copy out there, somewhere!

Shakespeare's death

After just a few years living back in Stratford, Shakespeare died, on 23 April 1616, thought to be his 52nd birthday. He is buried in Stratford's Holy Trinity Church, with an epitaph warning that his grave and body must never be moved:

Good friend for Jesus sake forbeare,
To dig the dust enclosed here.
Blessed be the man that spares these stones,
And cursed be he that moves my bones.

GLOSSARY

alliteration	Grouping together words with the same initial letter
assonance	Grouping together words that sound similar
avenge	To take revenge on
blank verse	Type of non-rhyming poetry used by Shakespeare
contend	To compete
dialogue	Lines of speech in a play
doomsday	The end of the world
dramatis personae	A list of characters in a play
heckle	To shout out at someone on a stage
humours	Four substances once thought to exist in the body
mason	A stoneworker
melancholy	Sadness or a despondent mood
metaphor	Describing something as another thing to compare them
playwright	A writer of plays
prose	Text written in ordinary sentences, not in verse
stage directions	Instructions for the actors in a play
supernatural	Magical, or beyond the laws of nature
superstitious	Fearing or believing in luck, magic or the supernatural
symbol	Something that stands for an idea or object
tapestry	A picture made of embroidered cloth

GLOSSARY OF SHAKESPEARE'S LANGUAGE

arms	weapons
away	let's go
foul	evil or dirty
jest	humour or joking around
mark	notice or watch carefully
matter	a problem
mirth	laughter, sense of humour
of late	recently
perchance	maybe
shipwright	shipbuilder
'tis	it is
wherefore	why

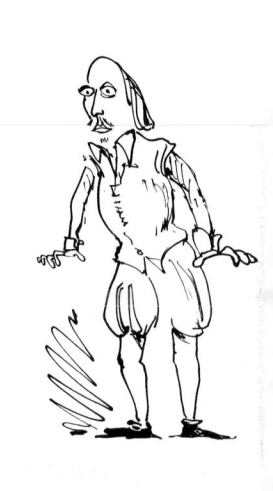

HAMLET QUIZ

Test yourself and your friends on
the story, characters and language
of Shakespeare's *Hamlet*. The answers
are at the bottom of the page.

1) Who saw the ghost before Hamlet did?
2) Where was the old king sleeping when he was murdered?
3) Name the prince of Norway who planned to attack Denmark.
4) Who is the father of Laertes and Ophelia?
5) Name the play Hamlet asked the actors about.
6) Why wouldn't Hamlet kill Claudius as he prayed?
7) Whose ship did Hamlet return to Denmark on?
8) What kind of tree did Ophelia fall from?
9) How did Laertes die?
10) What were Hamlet's last words?

10) *The rest is silence.*
9) *He was cut by his own poisoned sword*
8) *A willow tree*
7) *The pirates' ship*
6) *Because he would go to heaven*
5) *The Murder of Gonzago*
4) *Polonius*
3) *Fortinbras*
2) *In the orchard*
1) *Barnardo, Marcellus and Horatio*

Short Sharp Shakespeare Stories

MACBETH
978 0 7502 8112 6

HAMLET
978 0 7502 8117 1

A MIDSUMMER NIGHT'S DREAM
978 0 7502 8113 3

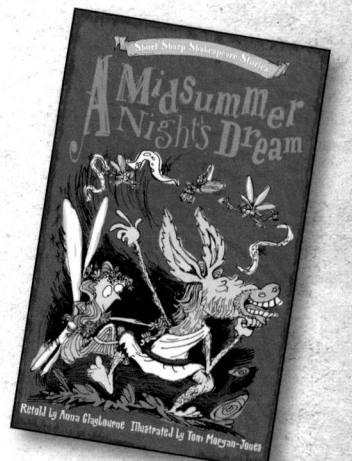

THE TEMPEST
978 0 7502 8115 7

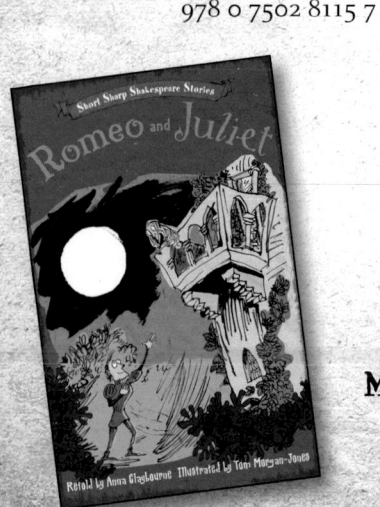

ROMEO AND JULIET
978 0 7502 8114 0

MUCH ADO ABOUT NOTHING
978 0 7502 8116 4